A GINGERBREAD CHRISTMAS

by TIM RAGLIN and ERIC METAXAS

RABBIT EARS

Library of Congress Catalog Card Number 91-15101

ISBN 0-688-11014-2

Printed in Singapore

Manufactured by Blaze Int'l Productions, Inc.

1 3 5 7 9 10 8 6 4 2

To P. J. Raglin—T.R.

To the Reason for the season—E.M.

It was Christmas Eve—the busiest day of the year for Santa Claus. As he went through the last-minute mail, he came upon a shocking letter. Santa immediately dropped what he was doing and went straight to the telephone. This was an emergency. Something had to be done right away.

Santa called his friends Spice and Ginger—the Prince and Princess of Gingerbread.

"Listen to this," he said when they answered. He read from the letter.

Dear Santa,
The mayor of our town has cancelled Christmas. What can we do? Please help us.
Yours truly,
A Concerned Citizen of Gloomsbury, USA

Ginger and Spice could hardly believe their ears. Cancel Christmas! Impossible!

Before hanging up, Santa asked to meet them at the train station.

"Prince and Princess of Gingerbread," said Santa when they got to the station. "As the Official Ambassadors of the North Pole, I hereby send you to the town of Gloomsbury. Your mission: Bring Christmas back to the town!"

"We won't let you down," said Spice.

"You can count on us," said Ginger.

And they set off toward the town of Gloomsbury.

When Spice and Ginger arrived in Gloomsbury, they could scarcely believe their eyes. There wasn't a Christmas decoration in sight.

"Everybody looks so unhappy," said Ginger.

"So it's true!" said Spice sadly. "They have really cancelled Christmas!"

"What's it to you, Doughboy?" said a surly voice from behind a newspaper. "The mayor says Christmas is a waste of time."

A little girl poked her head out.

"Have a candy cane," said Ginger, taking one from her suitcase.

The girl looked suspiciously at the candy cane. "My name is Hank," she said, "and I can't eat candy canes. They're illegal."

"Well, Merry Christmas, anyway!" called Ginger and Spice. They set off to begin their work.

Ginger and Spice had their work cut out for them. The Mayor of Gloomsbury, Franklin P. Fussbudget, believed that he was helping the town by outlawing Christmas. After all, holiday celebrations took up valuable time—time that might be better spent working.

"Chief O'Hara," he said to the police chief, "I order you to arrest anyone who celebrates Christmas. Get to work!"

"Yes, sir," said Chief O'Hara.

Meanwhile, Ginger and Spice went into a grocery store. "Merry Christmas!" they shouted. They tried to give out candy canes. But no one wanted any.

"Get that thing away from me!" said an old lady.

"But this is from Santa Claus!" said Spice.

"And it's Christmas!" said Ginger.

"Quiet!" said the woman. "We don't have Christmas in Gloomsbury anymore."

"Hand them over!" said the store manager, grabbing the bag. But Ginger and Spice held on tight. They pulled the bag back and forth. Finally it burst open, scattering candy canes everywhere!

Chief O'Hara came into the store. "You two are under arrest!" he said to Ginger and Spice.

"Under arrest!" they cried in alarm. The Prince and Princess turned and ran as fast as they could.

Ginger and Spice ducked into the Gloomsbury Zoo, hoping to find a place to hide. Chief O'Hara followed closely behind them. They ran through a crowd of spectators and came to the polar bear's cage—a dead end.

THALARCTOS
MARITIMUS

"I've got you two cookies cornered!" yelled the police chief who was
coming closer and closer. The Prince and Princess backed against the
bars. They were trapped! Just then, two white paws grabbed them and
pulled them into the cage.

"Mr. Ralph!" cried Ginger with delight. "It is good to see you!"

"Good to see you, too, Ginger and Spice," said the bear.

Chief O'Hara saw that the bear held the Gingerbreads in his arms. "You caught the criminals!" he cried. "Good work, Ralph."

"They are not criminals," said Ralph. "They're old friends of mine from the North Pole—the Prince and Princess of Gingerbread."

"We have come to wish you Merry Christmas," said Ginger.

"But Christmas is against the law," said the police chief.

Ralph laughed. "That's what you think. Take it away, kids!"

Ginger and Spice joined Ralph the polar bear in a Christmas jig. Soon
everyone, including Chief O'Hara, was dancing, laughing, and clapping.
They were beginning to get in the Christmas spirit—law or no law.
For giving such a wonderful performance, Ginger, Spice, and Ralph

were given three tickets to the opera that night. In return, Ginger and Spice gave candy canes to everyone.

But when Mayor Fussbudget heard what had happened at the zoo, he grew red with rage. "Those two cookies must be stopped!"

When Ginger and Spice arrived at the opera house, they were surprised to find that the star singer was Madame Bubbles Tonsilopovich, their very own childhood baby-sitter! After her final aria, the Prince, the Princess, and Ralph the polar bear joined her on stage.

"Citizens of Gloomsbury!" called Spice. "Merry Christmas!"

"You can't say that!" cried someone in the audience. "It is against the law. Christmas has been cancelled!"

"You cannot cancel Christmas!" said Ginger. "Christmas is a warm and joyous spirit. It is how we feel toward one another."

The audience argued and jeered. No one seemed to care that it was already Christmas Eve.

Just then, Madame Tonsilopovich whispered something to Ginger, Spice, and Ralph. Then the four of them began singing the jolly National Anthem of the North Pole.

Soon, the people in the audience stopped yelling and began to listen. Before long, everyone was dancing in the aisles. It was Christmas Eve! And it felt so good to celebrate!

Everyone was happy—except for the mayor, who was watching from the wings. He was so angry that he went onstage and arrested Spice and Ginger!

"Boo!" cried the audience. "Boooo!"

"The next person who boos is under arrest!" said the mayor.

Everyone stopped booing—except for one small voice in the crowd. "BOO!"

"Who did that?" The mayor peered into the audience. The person kept on booing. And then the mayor saw who it was—it was Hank!

"Henrietta Fussbudget!" said the mayor. "What are you doing here?"

"Please don't arrest them, Daddy," cried Hank. "It's Christmas!"

Ginger and Spice looked at each other in surprise. Hank was the daughter of Mayor Fussbudget!

"Why aren't you home doing your homework?" said the mayor.

"I already did my homework," said Hank.

"Then do it again," said Mayor Fussbudget. "It is *not* Christmas! Christmas has been cancelled!" And he led Ginger and Spice away.

As Mayor Fussbudget led Ginger and Spice to the jail house, he came upon a big crowd in the square outside City Hall. The people of Gloomsbury had come to help Ginger and Spice. They wanted to celebrate Christmas Eve.

"What's going on?" the mayor said angrily. "Arrest the whole town, O'Hara!"

But just then they heard a sweet, jingling sound. It was soft at first, but it grew louder as it came closer. It was Santa Claus!

"Ho ho ho!" cried Santa as he landed his sleigh. "Merry Christmas!"

"What should we do now, Mayor Fussbudget?" said Chief O'Hara. The mayor sighed deeply. "Just say 'ho,' O'Hara."

"Merry Christmas!" said Santa. "One of your citizens sent me a letter alerting me that you had cancelled Christmas. But it looks like Ginger and Spice have straightened things out."

The mayor blushed. "I see that cancelling Christmas was a big mistake. Would the person who sent the letter please step forward so I can say thanks." A murmur went through the crowd. Who had sent the letter?

"I sent the letter, Daddy," said a voice. It was Hank, the mayor's own daughter.

"You!" cried the mayor in surprise. "Why—"

Santa smiled. "She has the Christmas spirit."

Mayor Fussbudget put his arm around Hank and smiled. "I sure am proud of you, Henrietta."

"Spice, Ginger, you did fine work," said Santa Claus. "But now we must be going. I've got quite a few more stops to make tonight!" Ginger and Spice climbed aboard the sleigh. "Good-bye!" they called. "And Merry Christmas!"

"Merry Christmas!" called all the people of Gloomsbury. Then they watched as Santa's sleigh took off into the starry night. Everyone felt warm and happy—even the mayor. Christmas had come, after all.